Ernie
& the
Big Newz

Ernie Anastos

with illustrations by Bill Gallo

Dedicated to every child in the world who has a dream.

This book will inspire you to follow your dream and become everything that is possible.
It is important to remember to do something that makes the world a better place.

A special thank you to my friend Bill Gallo,
celebrated *Daily News* columnist, for illustrating this dream.

—Ernie Anastos

The Make-A-Wish Foundation® of America,
an important organization that helps
make children's wishes come true, will receive
two dollars from the sale of each book.
To learn more, visit: www.wish.org

Drawings by Bill Gallo,
celebrated *Daily News* illustrator

Copyright © 2007 by New World Books
In association with NK Publications, Inc.
www.nkpublications.com
P. O. Box 1735, Radio City Station
New York, New York 10101

Ernie and the Big Newz is a registered trademark
www.ErnieandtheBigNewz.com.

ISBN 10: 0-9705100-5-5
ISBN 13: 978-0-9705100-5-1

This book is about a youngster who followed his dream and became a TV reporter in New York City. Consider what you would like to do when you grow up. What is your dream? What are your special interests and talents? Most importantly, think about how to use your gifts to make that dream come true.

If you have ever thought of becoming a television news reporter, then this book will help you. www.ErnieandtheBigNewz.com is a special website about this book and about Ernie Anastos. As a top TV news anchor and reporter in New York City, he has some helpful advice about beginning an exciting career in television journalism. We want to see you reporting the news on TV someday soon!

Visit us at:

www.ernieandthebignewz.com

Meet Ernie!

Ever since he was a little boy, Ernie dreamed of being a television news reporter. When he was only ten years old, he built a make believe radio studio in the basement of his house. He hung white bed sheets from the ceiling pipes, like a tent. He wrote, "Ernie's News" on the top part of the sheets and set up a desk and a play microphone in front. From here, Ernie could report the latest news to his neighborhood friends.

"Mandy's Candies" is out of Fudgesicles today," Ernie announced to his basement audience.

"Mr. Grigas, the mailman, slipped on the ice and hurt his ankle. Dr. Lewkowitz says the flu is getting bad." Ernie kept his friends and neighbors up-to-date on all that was happening. His radio broadcasts were a hit!

As Ernie was growing up, he read newspapers everyday. He listened to the radio and watched the news on TV. He loved knowing about the different things that were happening in his city and around the world.

In school, Ernie started a current events club. At the meetings, Ernie and his classmates would talk about different news stories they had read or heard. They would share the most interesting and unusual stories about different people and distant places. It was fun!

Ernie knew that someday he would be a real TV news reporter.
"I can't wait!" he would say to himself. Ernie was young, though, and he
needed experience. When he was sixteen, he landed a job as a disc jockey at
his hometown radio station, WOTW. Lowering his voice to sound older and
more mature, Ernie would announce, "Hi, everyone, it's bright and sunny
today and 68 degrees."

The best part of his job was when he read the news on the radio.

Through high school and college, Ernie worked at different radio stations.
He learned how important it is to make sure every fact is accurate before
reporting a story on the news. Ernie was getting a lot of good experience
while he was still dreaming about being a television news reporter.

Then one day Ernie got his big break! He was offered a job as a TV reporter
for the popular Big Newz team in New York City where 8-million people live
and work. Ernie's own hard work had paid off. His dream was coming true.
He was ready and there were so many stories to tell!

So, come along with Ernie as he begins his adventures as a reporter for Big
Newz, covering some BIG stories.

Ernie's first day as a news reporter was Thanksgiving Day. He was going to cover the famous Macy's Thanksgiving Day Parade! Thousands and thousands of people across the country watch this exciting New York parade each year. The long line of marching bands and enormous floats winds through New York City. It entertains millions of excited onlookers bundled in warm jackets and colorful scarves against the cold November winds. Best of all are the huge, huge balloons of famous cartoon characters and heroes that bob high in the air winking and smiling at the crowds below.

Hovering above the crowds and the balloons was the Big Newz Skycopter. Inside, Ernie held the microphone and Ardina, his partner, held the camera. The pilot kept the skycopter moving along with the parade below.

Ernie and Ardina had a hard time holding the microphone and camera steady as the small helicopter bounced in the windy sky.

Ernie popped a tiny earpiece into his right ear so that he could hear Ron, the TV director, in the control room of the studio. "Standby," Ron whispered into Ernie's ear.

"Five seconds, four, three, two, one...

and you're on the air!"

The small red tally light on Ardina's camera blinked and Ernie clicked on his microphone. "Happy Thanksgiving!" he eagerly began his first report. "This is Ernie live in the Big Newz Skycopter over the Macy's Parade."

Ernie watched the movement below and kept reporting, "There are thousands of people gathered today to see the colorful floats, unusual balloons, and bands from all different parts of the country. We're watching Lady Liberty, Tom the Turkey, and even Santa Claus passing by right now! Stay tuned for more...now, back to our studio."

11

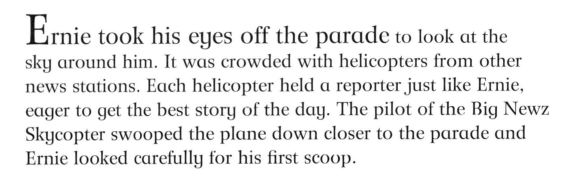

Ernie took his eyes off the parade to look at the sky around him. It was crowded with helicopters from other news stations. Each helicopter held a reporter just like Ernie, eager to get the best story of the day. The pilot of the Big Newz Skycopter swooped the plane down closer to the parade and Ernie looked carefully for his first scoop.

Ernie marveled at all the colors and energy below. He noticed the serious faces on the mounted police officers lining the length of the parade route. Each rider sat straight on a brown or gray horse, keeping order amid the excitement.
Ernie also noticed that the Big Newz Skycopter ride was becoming bumpy. Snowflakes were beginning to swirl around the bouncing 'copter.

Then something happened.

Ernie saw that the Candy Cane float had suddenly come to a stop, holding back the rest of the parade. The children aboard the striped float were laughing and pointing at something in the street. Ernie could see that a little spotted brown and white puppy was running around right in the middle of the street. This looked like breaking news!

"Bring the 'copter down closer," Ernie told the pilot. "Ardina, get your camera rolling!"
The unleashed pup seemed to be barking orders to the halted parade and thoroughly enjoying the attention of all the parade goers.

Television viewers were watching the action live from Ardina's camera. "We have a newsbreak, ladies and gentlemen," Ernie reported. "If you can believe it, a small puppy has run out in front of the Candy Cane float and has managed to stop the parade!"

People at home were treated to a remarkable sight as they watched the spectators laughing and pointing at the frisky pup. They listened to Ernie's upbeat reporting, "This puppy is running the show and is starring in his own role in the Thanksgiving Day Parade!"

Ardina's camera zoomed in on one of the mounted police trying to approach the lively dog. Each time the horse and rider neared, the puppy dashed off in a new direction, commanding more laughter from the crowds.

Ernie continued, "The puppy's part in the parade is almost over, folks. A police officer is scooping up the mischievous dog and carrying it off safely to the sideline. Look at the applauding, cheering crowd!"

Laughing with his pals in the Skycopter, Ernie concluded, "Everyone is OK, the puppy is in the arms of a smiling mounted police officer, and the extraordinary Macy's Parade is continuing down Broadway!"

Ernie was the first reporter on the scene with the story. He had his first scoop!

The snow was coming down harder. It was time to fly the Big Newz Skycopter back to the heliport on West 30th Street. "After we land," Ernie suggested to Ardina, "let's go over to Times Square and see if anything is happening."

As the Skycopter headed to its base, Ernie called the Big Newz weather center. Their report was not good: an unexpected, nasty snowstorm was on the way. Ernie arranged for another Thanksgiving Day broadcast, this time from one of New York City's busiest intersections.

"Let's go over to Times Square and see if anything is happening."

When the news duo arrived at Times Square, the Big Newz Van was in place, raising its tall, metal antenna through the thickening snow, into the sky, ready to broadcast. Ernie buttoned his wool coat more tightly around his cold neck and brought the collar up around his reddening ears. He watched for the tally light to flash on Ardina's camera and waited for the countdown from Ron.

"This is Ernie reporting live from Times Square." Brushing heavy, white snowflakes away from his eyes, Ernie continued, "The holiday weather forecast is for lots of snow. Traveling will be difficult and the roads will be slippery; it's going to be a long, cold night. Be careful!"

Ardina's camera was capturing scenes of trashcans toppling while papers, hats, and wrappers were being swept through the streets by angry winds.

"The holiday forecast is calling for lots of snow!"

Ernie heard his cell phone ring. "This is Ron. We just got a tip from a viewer in Westchester County. There has been a bad car accident on Route 22. Take the Big Newz Van and get to the scene. No one else has the story yet."

"We're on it!"
As the van headed north into the worsening storm, Ernie asked Ron to give him all the facts.

A woman had been driving with her 8-year-old son when suddenly the car skidded off the icy road into a ditch. The mother was trapped inside the car, but the frightened, young boy had escaped and ran for help. Ernie knew that this was breaking news. He was anxious to get to the scene.

By the time Ernie, Ardina, and the Big Newz Van arrived, there was action and excitement at the site. Police cars with brightly flashing lights were lining the road. Firefighters carrying heavy rescue equipment were rushing to the overturned car. An ambulance was standing by with an emergency team ready.

The Big Newz van raced to the scene.

Ernie and Ardina jumped from the van and ran to the side of the road overlooking the scene of the crash. Ernie immediately began to write facts on his notepad as Ardina got her video camera rolling, taping all the activity. Ernie saw the nametag on the firefighter standing beside him and asked, "Chief Malloy, do you know yet if everyone is OK?" Ardina was picking up the live interview on camera.

"It really is a miracle," the chief answered, pointing to the car. "We were able to pull the driver out safely. She was injured, but not seriously. The young boy, Andy, called for help. He saved his mother's life!"

Ernie immediately began to write facts on his notepad as Ardina got her video camera rolling.

"I ran as fast as I could to get help."

Ernie wanted to find Andy and include him in his broadcast. This, he knew, was a great story. Then he spotted Andy standing beside a police officer, who was bending to speak with the boy at eye-level. Ernie walked toward them, continuing his live broadcast; Ardina followed, camera rolling.

"Andy, can I talk with you for a minute? You're a hero!" The young boy smiled.
"Can you tell us exactly what happened?" Ernie lowered the microphone close to the boy's mouth.

There was a pause, then Andy spoke clearly, "Everything happened so fast! Once the car stopped sliding, I saw that my mom was hurt and couldn't get out, but I could. I pushed hard on the door on my side until it opened enough for me to crawl out. Then I ran as fast as I could to that house over there. I banged on the door and the lady who answered called the police for me." Ardina was capturing a close-up of the boy then she panned to the house across the road. "I just hope my mom is OK," Andy whispered, looking at Ernie.

Before Ernie could speak, the sound of clapping came from the side of the road where the ambulance stood. Andy's mother was moving quickly to her son. She grabbed him and held him in a tight hug. Then she kissed the top of his snow-covered cap.

Ardina had it all on camera. "This, ladies and gentlemen," said Ernie looking into the camera, "is a happy ending!" He looked at Andy, who was smiling up at his mom and continued, "Andy, your family can end this Thanksgiving Day giving thanks to you, its hero!"

Ernie turned. The camera had Andy, his mom, and many of the police and firefighters in the background. Ardina zoomed in on Ernie's face. "I'm your Big Newz reporter, Ernie, and that's tonight's BIG story. Happy Thanksgiving, everybody!"

It was time to head back to the newsroom.

"This, ladies and gentlemen, is a happy ending!"

There was cheering for Ernie and Ardina when they entered the office. Ernie had reported not one, but TWO scoops on his very first day as a television reporter for Big Newz! Ernie knew he was meant to be a reporter. He loved his new job.

Most importantly, Ernie knew there would be lots more stories to share with his viewers and he would have many more adventures covering The Big Newz!

"Ernie Anastos, you're the greatest! You have achieved many accomplishments during your illustrious career."
—Walter Cronkite, *celebrated CBS News anchor*

"Ernie is a legend in television news. I should know, I sit next to him every night."
—Rosanna Scotto, *co-anchor Fox 5 News*

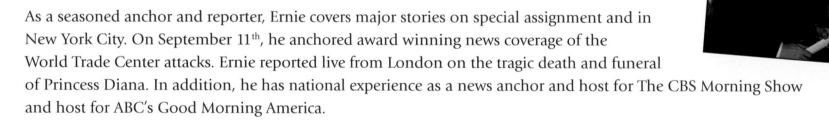

ERNIE ANASTOS is a premier news anchor with more than 25 years experience and is recognized in the New York State Broadcaster's Hall of Fame. He has won 30 Emmy awards and nominations, including "Best Newscast in New York" and the prestigious Edward R. Murrow award for excellence. Throughout the years, he has gained wide popularity and respect within New York City's uniquely diversified community, nurturing a sense of trust and confidence among viewers.

As a seasoned anchor and reporter, Ernie covers major stories on special assignment and in New York City. On September 11th, he anchored award winning news coverage of the World Trade Center attacks. Ernie reported live from London on the tragic death and funeral of Princess Diana. In addition, he has national experience as a news anchor and host for The CBS Morning Show and host for ABC's Good Morning America.

As a Phi Kappa Phi honoree, Ernie graduated summa cum laude with a Bachelor of Arts degree from Northeastern University where he is a noted member of the university corporation. His academic credits include graduate studies at Columbia University and he also holds an Honorary Doctorate degree in Humanities.

Ernie is a celebrated author, most recently introducing this series of children's books titled, *Ernie and the Big Newz*. Previously, he wrote an historical book on the lifestyle of America's youth. *Twixt: Teens Yesterday and Today,* was featured at the Smithsonian in Washington, D.C. and in *The New York Times*. He has also been a contributing columnist for *Family Circle*, the world's largest selling women's magazine.